Other Books by Elizabeth Levy/Mordicai Gerstein

Something Queer Is Going On

Something Queer at the Ballpark

Nice Little Girls

Weekly Reader Books presents

(a mystery)

something queer at the Library

by
Elizabeth Levy
illustrated by
Mordicai Gerstein

Delacorte Press, New York

Library of Congress Cataloging in Publication Data

Levy, Elizabeth.
Something queer at the library.

SUMMARY: Gwen and Jill's discovery of some
mutilated library books strangely links up with a
dog show in which they entered their dog.
[1. Mystery and detective stories] I. Gerstein,
Mordicai. II. Title.
PZ7.L5827Sn   [E]   76-49906
ISBN 0-440-08127-0
ISBN 0-440-08128-9 lib. bdg.

This book is a presentation of
Weekly Reader Books.
Weekly Reader Books offers
book clubs for children from
preschool to young adulthood. All
quality hardcover books are selected
by a distinguished Weekly Reader
Selection Board.

For further information write to:
Weekly Reader Books
1250 Fairwood Ave.
Columbus, Ohio 43216

"The All-State Dog Show is next week," Jill explained to Mr. Hobart, the librarian. "We're going to show Fletcher. He's a pure-bred basset hound, but he's never been in a dog show. We need these books to learn how to train him."

"They're oversized books. Usually, I'd ask you to read them here," said Mr. Hobart. "But we're about to close, so I'll let you sign them out for one week. You must take good care of them."

"We promise," said Gwen and Jill.

"I can trust you," said Mr. Hobart. "Good luck!"

FLETCHER'S
TAIL WAGGING →

Fletcher was sleeping under a tree outside the library. Gwen and Jill untied him and hurried home. Fletcher didn't want to hurry. Fletcher never wanted to hurry.

When they got home, Fletcher went to sleep again. Gwen and Jill opened the books.

"Look!" cried Jill. "Somebody's cut out a picture."

"Some pictures are missing in this one, too," said Gwen.

Quickly they leafed through the other books. In each one, a few pictures were cut out. "This is terrible!" said Jill. "What a horrible, creepy thing to do!"

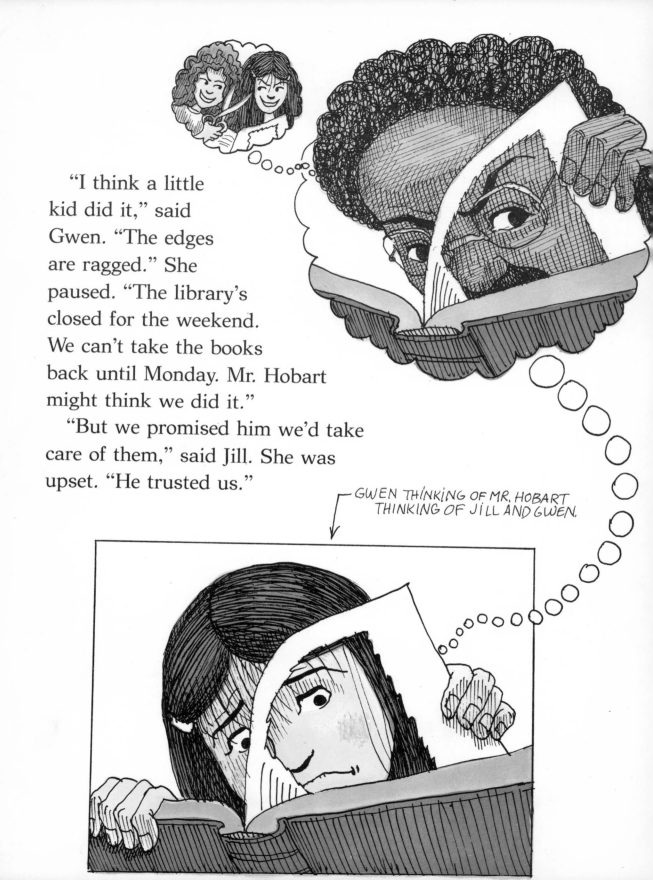

"I think a little kid did it," said Gwen. "The edges are ragged." She paused. "The library's closed for the weekend. We can't take the books back until Monday. Mr. Hobart might think we did it."

"But we promised him we'd take care of them," said Jill. She was upset. "He trusted us."

GWEN THINKING OF MR. HOBART THINKING OF JILL AND GWEN.

Gwen looked at the books on the floor. Then she looked at Jill. "We're going to have to catch the creep who did this ourselves." Gwen started to tap her braces. She always tapped her braces whenever something queer was going on. "I bet there's a clue in the books somewhere," she said.

TAP TAP TAP TAP TAP TAP TAP TAP

GWEN, TAPPING ON THOSE ⟶ BRACES

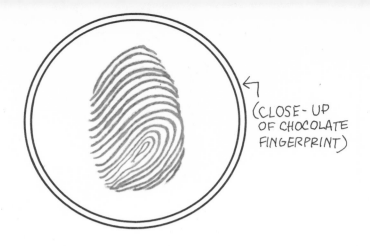

(CLOSE-UP
OF CHOCOLATE
FINGERPRINT)

They went over the books page by page.
"I found something," shrieked Jill. "A
fingerprint! The creep was eating chocolate and left a fingerprint. You can see
the swirls. We've got him—or her."

(NOT A GOOD CLUE)

"Jill," said Gwen. "A fingerprint doesn't do us any good. We're not the police."

"We could take it to them," insisted Jill.

"It doesn't prove anything. It could have been left by anybody. There must be more clues. Let's keep looking."

A half hour went by, but they didn't find anything. Then Gwen yelled, "Look at this!" She pointed to a strange drawing of a dog on the margin of the page.

CLOSE-UP OF FUNNY LOOKING DRAWING

"It's silly looking," said Jill.

"It's a better clue than the fingerprint," said Gwen, tapping her braces. "I bet whoever did it always draws dogs like that. We'll trace it on a piece of paper and ask if anybody has seen a drawing like it before."

HAL

PAT

LIZ

ALAN

Gwen and Jill showed the drawing to all of their friends.

They looked at all the art work on the walls in school.
Nothing matched the dog doodle.

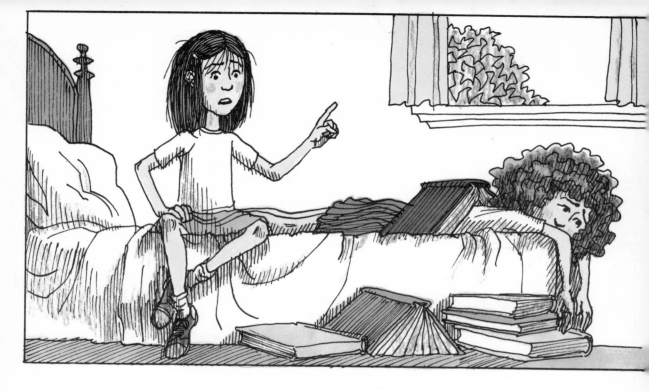

By Wednesday, they had made no progress.

"It's hopeless," said Jill.

"But we can't give up," said Gwen.

"What about the dog show?" asked Jill. "We haven't even started to train Fletcher. If he wins, at least we'll have money to pay for the books."

"We shouldn't have to pay," said Gwen angrily. "The creep who did it should pay."

Gwen and Jill tried to teach Fletcher how to behave at a dog show. He was supposed to stand straight with his nose in the air.

He was supposed to run at Jill's side in a steady gait.

When Fletcher tried to stand, his nose and belly drooped.

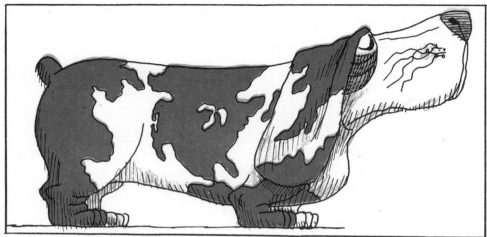

THE RIGHT WAY

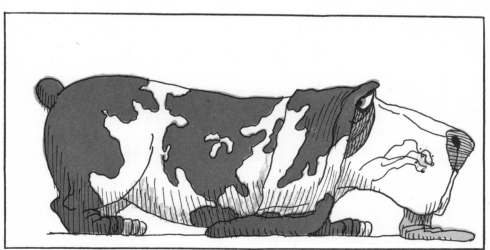

FLETCHER'S WAY

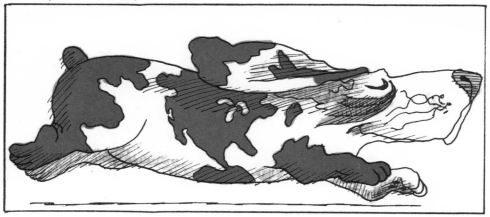

He kept tripping when he tried to run.
Fletcher was very good at lying down on command.

On Friday, Gwen said, "It's no use. Fletcher will never win."

"Basset hounds are supposed to droop," said Jill, trying to sound hopeful.

Gwen shook her head back and forth. "To-morrow, after the dog show, we have to take the books back to Mr. Hobart. He'll think we did it. This has been one of the worst weeks of my life!"

"Maybe we missed something in the books," suggested Jill. "Let's look again."

Gwen shrugged her shoulders,
but they went inside and looked at
each book. Suddenly Gwen began
to go tap,

        tap,

           tap on her braces.

"You've found something," cried Jill.

"Look at the captions underneath each missing picture," said Gwen. "They all say Lhasa apso. Sounds like a weird dog food. Do you know what it is?"

"I never heard of it," said Jill.

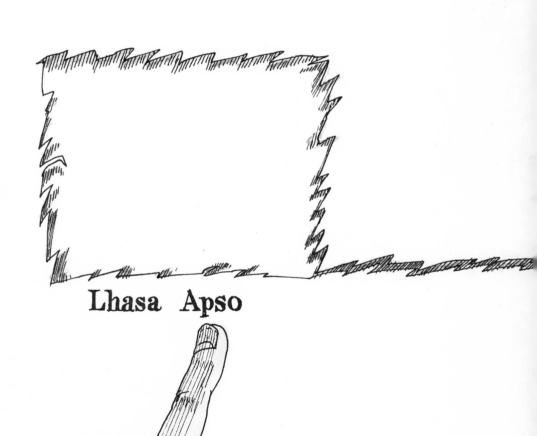

Lhasa Apso

"We've got to find out. Let's go to the library," said Gwen.

They ran all the way. Fletcher was exhausted when they got there.

"Hi, Gwen and Jill," said Mr. Hobart when he saw them. "Did you bring back the books?"

"They're not due till tomorrow," said Gwen, turning a deep red.

"Is there something wrong?" asked Mr. Hobart. He looked puzzled.

"Oh no," stammered Gwen. "We just have to look something up in the encyclopedia."

"Now he'll really suspect us," whispered Jill. "Why did you have to turn all red?"

"I couldn't help it," whispered Gwen.

THE CITY OF LHASA

LHASA APSO

They got the L volume and looked up Lhasa. It was the capital of Tibet. They found out that Lhasa apso was a funny-looking little dog that originally came from Tibet. Apso meant barking lion in the Tibetan language, so Lhasa apso was a tiny barking lion from Tibet.

A SMALL LION   A LARGE LHASA APSO

Gwen sat down on the floor between the stacks and started tapping her braces. "Let's make a list of everything we know about the creep," she said.

1. eats chocolate (maybe)
2. draws dog doodles
3. cuts out pictures of Lhasa apsos

the creep....
①eats chocolate
(maybe)
②draws dog
~~d~~oodles
③cuts out
pictures of
Lhasa
Apsos

↳ GWEN'S NOTES

"The dog show!" shouted Gwen.

"Shhh," said Jill. "We're in the library. What about the dog show?"

"Those lopsided whatchamacallits will be at the dog show," explained Gwen. "I bet the creep will be there, too!"

A LOPSIDED LHASA APSO

The next morning was the start of the dog show. Gwen and Jill gave Fletcher a bath. They combed and brushed him, and practiced running him around in a circle.

Then they hurried to the show.

DOG SHOW

When they got there, Gwen said, "You stay with Fletcher. I'm going to look around. Keep your eye out for any kids eating chocolate."

Gwen found the section reserved for Lhasa apsos. After a while a boy came by eating chocolate raisins. His fingers were covered with chocolate. Gwen started to follow him and almost bumped into a girl eating a Three Musketeers candy bar. Her hands were smeared with chocolate, too.

Gwen didn't know what to do. The girl stopped and looked at the Lhasa apsos. The boy started to walk away. The girl took out a pad and pencil. Quickly, Gwen went over to the girl.

"Nice drawing," Gwen said as the girl began to doodle.

"Thanks," said the girl with a sigh.

"What's your name?" asked Gwen.

← THE DOODLE THAT GWEN TRACED FROM THE BOOK

"Pam." She sighed again. "I love Lhasa apsos. My aunt has one, but my parents won't let me have a dog."

"Gee, Pam, that's too bad," said Gwen. "Is that why you cut their pictures out of library books?"

Pam turned green. She dropped her
pad and pencil and ran.

"Hey, come back," cried Gwen. She
ran after her.

"Jill! Jill!! I found her. HELP!"

Jill came running, dragging Fletcher behind her. They chased the girl all over the dog show, past the Irish setters, the Old English sheepdogs and Airedales.

FLETCHER

JILL

IRENE   DON

GWEN

PAM

DICK

GAIL   CATLIN

(GWEN'S SHOE CAME UNTIE

JASON

ANKE

ANNIS

THERE GOES PAM

HAL

JILL

FLETCHER GETS TANGLED

GWEN BUMPS INTO A MAN

HERE'S PAM

They cornered her next to the fox terriers.

"You cut those pictures out of the library books," accused Gwen. "That's against the law."

"And a creepy, selfish thing to do," said Jill.

"I couldn't help myself," said Pam. "My parents got so sick of hearing me ask for a dog that they wouldn't even buy me a book with pictures of dogs. So I started going to the library. First, I was going to cut out just one little picture for my wall, then…"

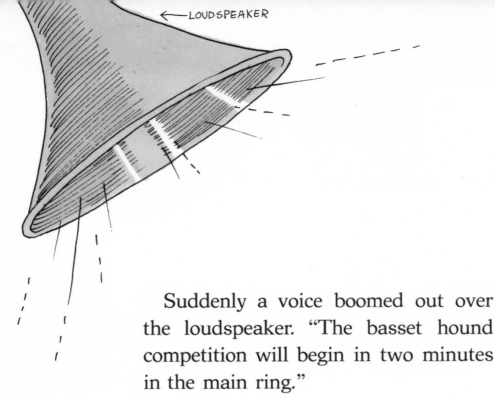

←—LOUDSPEAKER

Suddenly a voice boomed out over the loudspeaker. "The basset hound competition will begin in two minutes in the main ring."

"Come on," yelled Jill, waking Fletcher up. They hurried to the main ring. They made Pam go with them.

Fletcher did not win first prize. The judge said his stomach slumped too much. However, he won $25 for the most unusual markings.

"Congratulations," Pam said shyly as Gwen and Jill came out of the ring. "I'm really sorry about the library books." Pam started to scratch the top of Fletcher's head.

"You really love dogs, don't you?" said Gwen.

"Fletcher's wonderful," said Pam. "I think basset hounds are almost as nice as Lhasa apsos."

Jill grinned.

That afternoon, Gwen and Jill took Pam, the books, and Fletcher to the library. Mr. Hobart was very serious. He told Pam her parents would have to pay for the books. He made her promise she would never cut a picture out of a library book again. Then Mr. Hobart went outside to look at Fletcher's award-winning markings. He was very impressed.

Later that afternoon, Pam went with Gwen, Jill, and Fletcher to a pet store. They bought Fletcher a water bed with the $25 he had won.

"I bet he's wanted that since he was a puppy," said Gwen as Fletcher fell asleep, slowly bobbing up and down in his new bed.

JILL, FILLING THE WATER BED

PAM

About the Author

ELIZABETH LEVY is the author of many books, among them *Nice Little Girls,* called "humorously accurate" by *School Library Journal.* The *Something Queer* series (*Something Queer Is Going On, Something Queer at the Ball Park,* and now *Something Queer at the Library*) has earned her the title "the Dorothy Sayers of the elementary set" (*Learning* magazine). Among her other books for young readers are *Lizzie Lies a Lot* and *Before You Were Three,* for which she was co-author with Robie H. Harris. Ms. Levy grew up in Buffalo, New York, and now lives in New York City, where she writes full time.

About the Artist

MORDICAI GERSTEIN is an animator and illustrator. His illustrations for *Something Queer Is Going On* were called "a sunny lark" by *Publishers Weekly,* and *School Library Journal* said about *Nice Little Girls,* "Gerstein's cartoons capture the world of playground and classroom with lighthearted deftness." His film fantasy for children, "The Magic Ring," won him a Cine Golden Eagle award. Mr. Gerstein grew up in California and now lives in New York City.

About the Book

The illustrations for this book were drawn with a Castel Faber fountain pen and Castel Faber TG pens of different sizes on Strathmore single ply kid finish paper. The color was done with paint and grease pencils on frosted acetate. The text has been set in 16 point Vladimir by Royal Composing Room.